ENCORE FOR ELEANOR

BILL PEET

Houghton Mifflin Company   Boston

With appreciation to
lots of terrific kids and
many a marvelous elephant

Library of Congress Cataloging in Publication Data

Peet, Bill.

Encore for Eleanor.

SUMMARY: Eleanor the elephant, a retired circus star, finds a new career as the resident artist in the city zoo.

[1. Elephants—Fiction. 2. Artists—Fiction]
I. Title.
PZ7.P253En [E] 80-15918
ISBN 0-395-29860-1

ISBN 0-395-29860-1 Reinforced Edition
ISBN 0-395-38367-6 Sandpiper Paperbound Edition

WOZ 20 19 18 17 16 15 14 13

Eleanor the elephant was a great circus star, and the one and only elephant ever to perform on a tall pair of stilts. The huge seven-ton pachyderm put on such a spectacular act that she always left the crowd calling for more.

"Encore! Encore!" everyone shouted. "Come on, Eleanor! Once more! Once more!"

But great circus stars can't keep going forever, no matter how clever they are, and after performing her act for over forty years, the old elephant was getting weak in the knees and was fearful of falling.

Then one summer night, while she was high up on her stilts, Eleanor suddenly lost her balance. Down she tumbled, to hit the sawdust floor in one colossal earthshaking "Ker Whump!" And as she lay there, sprawled out in a heap, a sudden hush fell over the crowd. Everyone thought surely the old elephant was done for, that she had broken every last bone.

But as it turned out, her worst injury was a slightly sprained ankle, and when she finally hauled herself onto her feet and went limping out of the big top, the crowd gave her a standing ovation.

Always before, the cheering of the crowd had been sweet music to Eleanor's big flappy ears, but nothing could make her happy on this

night. She was much too worried about what Colonel T. J. Tingle-hoffer, the circus boss, was thinking. Old T. J. expected everyone in his show to put on a top-notch performance, without so much as one little slip. So Eleanor was pretty sure that her dreadful crash landing was the very last act of her circus career.

Sure enough, T. J. decided that Eleanor was no longer fit to stay in the show.

"She's too much of a risk," he said. "The next time she falls, the old girl might flatten a clown or squash the ringmaster. She's just *got* to go."

So the very next day a seven-ton truck came to the circus grounds to haul Eleanor away. As she was about to leave, a few old friends were there to express their regrets and wish her the best wherever she went. And the unhappy elephant bade them farewell with a halfhearted wave of her trunk.

The next thing she knew, Eleanor was caught up in a great rush of traffic, jolting along through a big city, past dreary factory buildings. Since no one had told her where she was going, the elephant could only guess. And all sorts of grizzly ideas popped into her head.

She wondered if she might be heading for a glue factory. Then she

wondered if they ever made elephant-skin shoes, or elephant-leather jackets. And still worse, she wondered if she might be ground up into seven tons of fertilizer. Eleanor was quaking with fright from her trunk to her toes when the truck finally slowed down to enter a tall gateway.

It was the gateway to the city zoo, which was the only place Colonel Tinglehoffer could think of where a worn-out old circus elephant could live happily ever after.

She was put into a pen with plenty of hay and a full water trough, and her elephant house was a neat red barn shaded by a sycamore tree.

"I'm lucky to be here," said Eleanor after taking a look around, "and yet I'll never be happy unless I can perform a few tricks, or do something clever to earn my keep."

When people stopped at her pen to stare at her, Eleanor felt silly just standing there with nothing to do but stare back at them. And without her fancy circus robe and feathery headdress she felt like an overgrown wrinkled ugly big bloop of a thing.

"If I can't look my best," she grumbled, "then I don't want to be seen at all."

10
89

So she stayed out of sight as best she could by hiding in her barn all through the day until the zoo was closed. Then when she was sure no one was around to watch, Eleanor came out for her evening meal of alfalfa, cabbage, broccoli, lettuce, and carrots.

It was a lonely miserable life for an elephant who loved cheering crowds, bright lights, and lots of excitement. And she would have gone on being miserable if someone hadn't happened along to change her dreary routine.

That someone was a teenage girl who came to the zoo to sketch the animals. She made such a racket setting up her easel on the sidewalk that she awakened Eleanor from her afternoon nap. And being ever so curious, the elephant leaned out of her barn door to see what the noise was about. She was even more curious when she discovered the girl just outside the fence getting ready to make a drawing. Eleanor had often wondered how people drew pictures, and this was her chance to find out.

Eleanor hoped the girl wouldn't mind if she watched for a minute or two. Just the same, she was taking no chances, so without making a sound she crept across her pen to the fence, where she peeked over the girl's shoulder.

One glance was enough for Eleanor to see the girl was drawing the rhino who lived in the pen just across the way.

With a few quick strokes of her charcoal she had outlined the sleepy half-open eye, the stumpy horn, the wrinkly snout, and the underslung jaw. And to the elephant's delight, she even put the tufts of hair on the tips of the ears.

The girl was determined to make her drawing as lifelike as possible, right down to the smallest detail. So every now and then she stopped to study the rhino and figure out where to put all the creases and folds in his leathery hide.

She was in a hurry to get finished before the drowsy old fellow roused himself out of his stupor and changed position. But by the time the girl was ready to sketch the hind legs and the last half of the rhino, he felt an itch coming on.

All at once, he flopped on the ground and began rolling over and over on his back, snorting furiously and kicking up his heels.

"Oh Phooey!" exclaimed the girl. "Now wouldn't you know it! Why couldn't that big oaf stay put for one more measly minute? The inconsiderate clod!"

With an angry shrug, she tossed her charcoal onto the sidewalk, then crumpled up her drawing, and flung it into a trash can. Then she wandered away to a shady knoll overlooking a lily pond to watch the ducks and swans.

The elephant was disappointed too, and she was about to head back to her barn when she discovered that the charcoal was within easy reach, and the sketch pad and easel were less than a trunk length away. Suddenly the elephant was inspired to draw a picture, and after a sneaky sidelong glance at the girl to make sure she was still watching the ducks and swans, Eleanor seized the charcoal in her trunk.

Without a second to lose, the elephant drew the very first thing that came to mind, the familiar face of Zonko the clown she remembered from the circus. To start off, she made two crisscrosses for eyes, scrawled a couple of silly eyebrows and a long pointed nose, then a crooked toothy grin.

The drawing was far better than Eleanor expected, and she was smiling to herself as she drew the big ears, scribbled some hair, and put a tall hat on his head. The elephant was nearly finished with her picture and was putting a few ruffles on the floppy clown collar when suddenly she was caught by surprise.

"Wowie!" cried the girl, pulling the drawing off of the sketch pad. "I can't believe it! You wonderful big beastie! You are really terrific! Just fabulous! Too much!" Then waving the clown drawing in the air, the girl shouted at the top of her voice, "Come look! Come look, everyone!! Come see what the elephant drew!! Come look!"

In no time at all she was surrounded by a swarm of school kids and their teacher, along with Mr. McJunkens, the zoo director, who knew everything there was to know about animals.

The kids and their teacher loved the idea that the elephant had drawn a picture, and they were bubbling with excitement until Mr. McJunkens stepped in to squelch them all.

89

"I hate to spoil your fun," he said, "but I'm afraid it is altogether impossible for an elephant to draw a picture. Even though Eleanor was once a clever circus performer, she is after all nothing more than a dumb animal."

No one likes to be called dumb, especially a super-intelligent elephant like Eleanor, and she was furious.

"A dumb animal, am I?" she grumbled into her trunk. "I'll show that uppity fellow a thing or two. Oh, indeed I will!"

Once again Eleanor gripped the charcoal in her trunk, and, as everyone watched in amazement, the riled-up elephant dashed off a portrait of a lion. It was old Maynard, another familiar face from the circus, scraggly mane, mournful eyes, whiskers, and all. And she finished the sketch in only seventeen seconds!

"St-st-st-stupendous!" stammered Mr. McJunkens. "Fantastic! Eleanor is a super-sensational elephant! If she can draw a clown and a lion, she can draw lots of things! What do you say we put on an elephant-drawing show?!"

"Terrific idea!" everyone happily agreed. And of course Eleanor was overjoyed at the chance to be a star performer once more.

In less than a week, a special stage was built for the show, and an extra-large easel was set up to hold extra-large sketch pads so that Eleanor could make extra-large drawings for hundreds of schoolchildren to see. And best of all, Eleanor was outfitted in a fancy new robe so she could look her loveliest while she was performing her act.

Eleanor's drawings could never be considered great art; yet as far as anyone knew, they were the best drawings ever made by an elephant. But for all the kids could see they were "plenty good," and even "super terrific," and at the end of each performance the children were always calling for more.

"Encore! Eleanor! Encore!" they shouted. "One more, Eleanor! Please! Draw one more!" which was sweet music to the happy old elephant's big flappy ears.